Char... Small... journal was found ......
on the ban... the river Wyr...
Lancashi... ...gland. No ...
came f... ...ow old it m...
... ...longer e...
... information as t...

Charlie Small, please contact the publishe...

NAME: Charlie Small

ADDRESS: Gorilla City, the Jungle,
somewhere

AGE: ~~Eight~~ 400 (maybe even more)

MOBILE: 0777 43...

SCHOOL: St Beckham's

THINGS I LIKE: Exploring, climbing trees,
collecting rocks and animal skulls,
playing computer games, mountain biking,
skateboarding, watching TV.

THINGS I HATE: Danny Rook (a bully),
liver and onions, St Beckham's

PUBLISHER'S NOTE

Charlie Small's journal was found washed

THE FIRST AMAZING, ASTONISHING, INCREDIBLE AND TRUE ADVENTURES OF ME!
(Charlie Small)

GORILLA CITY

RED FOX

THE AMAZING ADVENTURES OF CHARLIE SMALL: GORILLA CITY
A RED FOX BOOK 978 1 782 95317 3

First published in Great Britain by David Fickling Books,
(when an imprint of Random House Children's Publishers UK
A Random House Group Company)

This Red Fox edition published 2014

5 7 9 10 8 6 4

**Penguin Random House is committed to a sustainable future for
our business, our readers and our planet. This book is made from
Forest Stewardship Council® certified paper.**

MIX
Paper from
responsible sources
FSC® C018179

Printed and bound in Great Britain by Clays Ltd, St Ives plc

Set in 15/17pt Garamond MT

Red Fox Books are published by Random House Children's Publishers UK,
61–63 Uxbridge Road, London W5 5SA

www.**randomhousechildrens**.co.uk
www.**totallyrandombooks**.co.uk
www.**randomhouse**.co.uk

Addresses for companies within The Random House Group Limited can be found at: www.
randomhouse.co.uk/offices.htm

THE RANDOM HOUSE GROUP Limited Reg. No. 954009

A CIP catalogue record for this book is available from the British Library.

If you find this book, PLEASE look after it. This is the only true account of my remarkable adventures.

My name is Charlie Small and I am at least four hundred years old. But in all those long years, I have never grown up. You see, something happened when I was eight. Something I can't begin to understand. I went on a journey... and I'm still trying to find my way home. And although I can now speak fluent gorilla, spit a hundred yards and swing through the canopy of a tropical rainforest, I still look like any eight-year-old boy you might pass in the street.

I've travelled to the ends of the earth and to the centre of the earth. I've fought giant crocodiles, challenged great apes and seen creatures you don't even know exist! You may think this sounds fantastic, you could think it's a lie, but you would be wrong. Because EVERYTHING IN THIS BOOK IS TRUE. Believe this single fact and you can share the most incredible journey ever experienced!

Charlie Small.

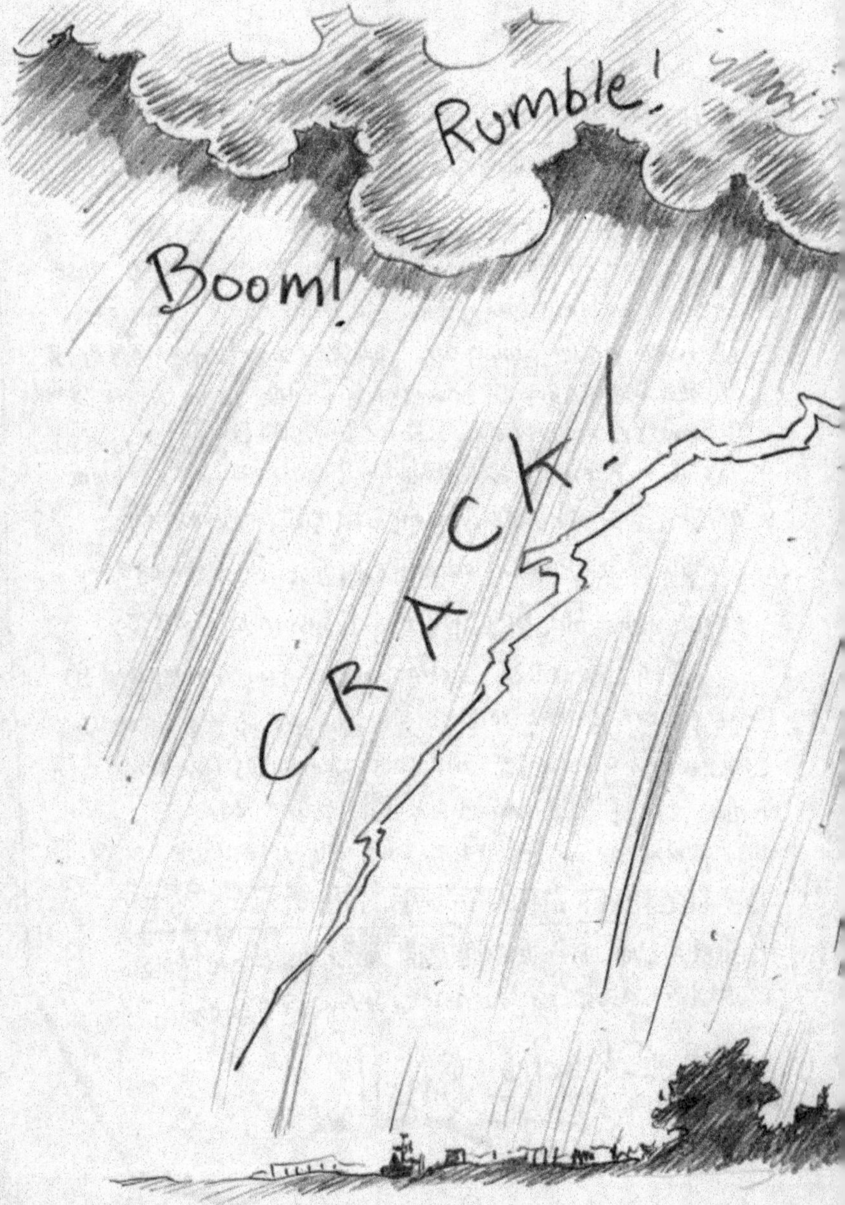
Rumble!
Boom!
CRACK!

My Adventures Begin

Such a lot has happened since lunchtime! It's now midnight and I'm camped in the middle of a vast and windswept plain, many miles from home. I'd been looking for adventure – and I've found it. More adventure than I could have possibly imagined!

It all started this afternoon. There was a huge storm last night and it was still raining really hard when I woke up, so I'd stayed indoors playing computer games. I'd finally beaten the big boss on level six when Mum came into my room.

'I can't believe you're still playing that stupid game, Charlie,' she sighed. 'It stopped raining ages ago. Why don't you go to the park? I'm sure some of your friends will be there.'

'I don't want to go to the park,' I said, pulling a face and striking the console with a rapid rat-a-tat-tat.

'You need some fresh air,' Mum insisted.

'But if I can just finish this next level, I'll beat my best score,' I protested.

Just then – and I have no idea what caused it – the computer crackled and a tiny spark of electricity ran a ragged path right across the picture. The game froze and the screen faded to black.

'No way!' I moaned. 'What was that?'

I tried rebooting the computer, but the game wouldn't restart. 'Oh, brilliant,' I scowled. 'It's broken! What am I supposed to do now?'

'Well,' said Mum, 'seeing as the computer is off and you don't want to go to the park, how about making yourself useful by tidying your room?'

I looked around at the huge piles of stuff on my floor and gulped. Suddenly going outside didn't seem like such a bad idea.

'Can't I go exploring, Mum?' I asked. 'If I promise to tidy my room later.'

Mum pursed her lips.

'I could try out that raft Dad helped me build . . .'

She put her hands on her hips.

'And you *did* say I needed some fresh air,' I pointed out.

'Oh, all right,' said Mum, heading downstairs with a sigh. 'Just don't be late for tea.'

Brilliant! I rummaged under my bed for my rucksack. I always took it out with me if I was going exploring, and kept it packed full of things that might come in handy.
Dragging it out, I
checked to make sure
they were all there:

1) My penknife (Mum
would kill me if she
knew about this!)
2) A ball of string
3) A water bottle (full)
4) A big bag of Paterchak's
mint humbugs (the stripy kind)
5) A telescope
6) My pyjamas (in case I ever have to camp out overnight!)
7) A scarf
8) An old railway ticket
9) This old notebook (to write up my adventures in)
10) My mobile phone and wind-up charger
11) A pack of wild animal collector's cards. They are full of very scary facts, and could be useful to an explorer

Humbugs
(very strong!)

COMPLIMENTARY

TICKET TO ANYWHERE
ONE WAY OR ANOTHER

DATE:
ANYTIME

16 2973

12) A glue pen (to stick any interesting finds in my book)

I swung the rucksack onto my back, threw my leg over the banister and slid down into the hall.

I'd just grabbed my coat and was running for the door when my nose caught the smell of freshly baked cakes wafting from the kitchen. I couldn't resist sneaking back to steal one off the tray.

'See you later, Mum,' I yelled, dodging past her and racing for the back door.

But if I'd known then what I know now, I would have grabbed the whole tray of cakes. Because something tells me I won't be tasting

Mum's delicious cooking again for a very long time.

But hold on! I'm getting ahead of myself! If this is to be a proper explorer's diary, I need to tell things in the right order. And that means I can't write about ~~██████~~ yet. (I want this to surprise you as much as it surprised me!) I need to explain how I got here, and why I don't think I'll be tasting any more of Mum's cakes any time soon . . .

I ran down the path to the bottom of our garden, pushed past the weeds at the side of the shed and stepped up onto the bank of the stream. I untied my raft, used the wooden oar to push my way through the reeds that grew thick from the bank, and began to paddle downstream. There was no one else around, but I didn't mind. I'd decided to see if I could make it all the way to the main river.

Up A Creek!

I soon realized that finding my way wasn't going to be easy. The stream was so full of rain from the thunderstorm that it had burst its banks. Muddy water was swirling through the reeds and tree roots at the bottom of next door's garden, and the waste-ground on the far bank was all flooded.

My little raft was soon bouncing about in the swirls and eddies, and twice I had to lean hard on my paddle so I wouldn't be tipped overboard. I was concentrating so hard I didn't notice that storm clouds were gathering in the sky once again.

It was then that things really started to happen . . .

There was a sudden rumble of thunder and the heavens opened. The rain came pouring down and I was soaked in seconds. The stream began churning with froth, and before I could paddle for the bank my raft was swept along in a surge of flood water!

It was pointless trying to paddle, so I raised the oar out of the water and *WHAM!* a huge bolt of lightning shot from the clouds. It flashed down onto the end of my upraised paddle and sent a judder dancing right through my body. Whoa! My limbs kicked and tingled with energy and then I was slammed down onto the raft as the fork of brilliant light passed right through me, fizzing and cracking along the stream until it disappeared from view.

I lay still for a moment as the raft spun in crazy circles, then I sat up very carefully, heart racing, and quickly inspected myself for damage. Amazingly I seemed to be completely unharmed!

I was just struggling to my feet when I heard a thick buzzing noise like a muffled chainsaw. I turned my head and *WHOOSH!* a huge dragonfly, much bigger than any I'd ever seen before, swooped past my nose and flew off across the reeds. I was so surprised I almost toppled into the water!

The dragonfly was as big as a crow!

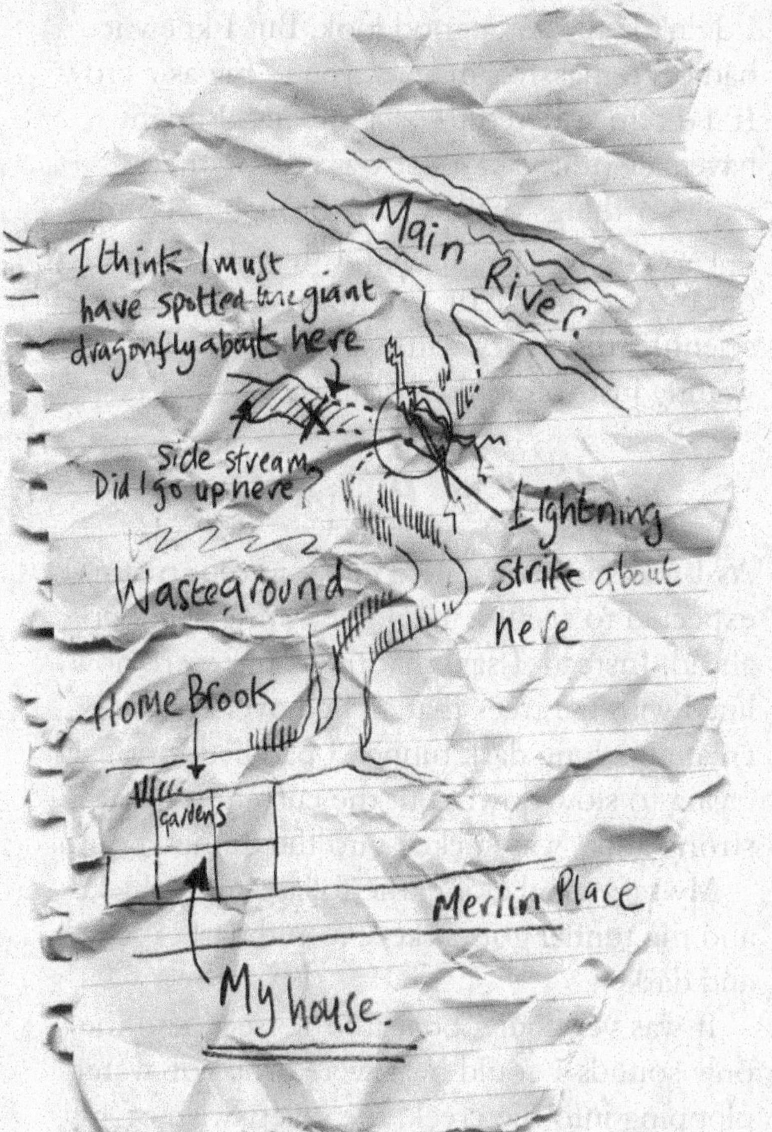

Main River
I think I must have spotted the giant dragonfly about here
Side stream. Did I go up here?
Lightning strike about here
Wasteground
Home Brook
gardens
Merlin Place
My house.

Don't forget net next time!

It was gone in a flash of emerald green, and I didn't really get a good look. But I knew it had been massive, maybe even as big as a crow. If I'd remembered to pack my net, I might have caught it. But a net was one of the explorer things that I hadn't brought with me.

I was a bit disappointed. I thought I'd missed out on the chance of making an important scientific discovery. Little did I know what was waiting just round the corner!

Into A Tunnel

As I was swept around a curve in the stream, I expected to see the main river somewhere up ahead. Instead, I saw that the banks were now lined with tall trees that arched over the water, creating a long dark tunnel. I paddled furiously, trying to slow down, but the current was too strong and I was sucked into the tunnel mouth.

My raft raced along, the foliage grew thicker and the tunnel got darker . . . and darker . . . and darker.

It was very quiet beneath the trees, and the only sounds I could hear were drops of water plopping into the creek, the quiet swish of my

The creek went into a
    tunnel of trees.

paddle as I tried to keep the boat steady, and—

Suddenly twigs cracked somewhere in the undergrowth and a strange cry came from the trees. I looked up in alarm and *SMACK* – an enormous cobweb caught me full in the face! It wrapped itself around my head, covering my eyes and filling my open mouth. It was as strong as cotton-thread and I had to tear at it with both hands to rip myself free.

Something dropped on to my shoulder and scuttled down my back. *Ugh!* I couldn't bear to look, but shook myself wildly until I heard whatever it was plop into the water behind me.

I sat back, panting hard, my heartbeat sounding loud amid the silence of the trees. This adventuring business was starting to get more than a little bit scary!

Part of me thought that perhaps I'd had enough exploring for one day, and that now was probably a very good time to go home. But what kind of an explorer would I be then? If every famous adventurer had run for home as soon as they'd got a fright, then nothing would ever have been discovered! No, I thought. A proper explorer would carry on – even if there were strange things lurking in the trees overhead.

The current was too strong for me to stop my raft anyway. And even if I could have slowed down, there was nowhere to climb out on to the bank. The sides of the stream were covered in a mass of thorny roots. I had to go on!

The entrance to the tunnel had now disappeared and I was in almost total darkness. I ducked low on my raft in case there were more cobwebs up ahead, and felt the stream twisting and turning as the current pulled me onwards. Pretty soon I had no idea which way was home.

'Don't panic,' I muttered to myself, starting to

panic. 'Don't— Whoa!'

Something nudged my raft, something *huge*, and I heard the slap of a tail on water. I paddled hard and fast, my heart pounding against my chest, and then, finally, I saw a pinprick of light in the distance. It looked like the end of the tunnel at last!

But just as I thought I might make it safely out at the other end, *CRUMP!* My raft was lifted out of the water and I toppled backwards, splashing into the river!

Danger From The Deep!

I sank in a cascade of bubbles, thrashing about in a blind panic. Through the churning water I glimpsed a cold black eye, then a row of teeth like chips of flint.

What was it?

Then, as I surfaced, I saw something rise near the far bank, and I knew: a CROCODILE!

But that was crazy! What was a crocodile doing in our local stream?

Now wasn't the time to wonder – the monster was speeding straight towards me, mouth wide open. Then, just as it closed in to strike, my raft drifted between us.

The crocodile took a huge bite, shaking the boat furiously until the ropes snapped and the logs splintered. Then it rolled, readying itself for another attack and, as its tail whipped past me, I grabbed hold, and hung on for dear life.

The croc started thrashing wildly, winding me and making me gasp. Then *WHOOSH,* we were away on a rollercoaster ride,

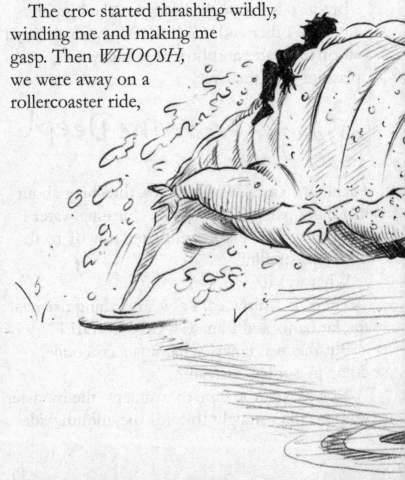

ploughing through the water and throwing up a huge fan of spray!

The crocodile twisted and turned, snapping at me as I clung desperately on. At one point I thought it was all over as the beast whipped round and slammed its mighty jaws shut. A powerful tug at my back nearly plucked me from my perch on its tail, and for one horrible moment I expected its rows of splintered teeth to slice into me. But then I realized that the beast had bitten into the rucksack on my back!

The enraged crocodile let go but continued to spin and spiral, leaping from the river, and then diving into its murky depths. Somehow I managed to hold on and crawl up its gnarled back, gripping its scaly body with my hands and knees like a bucking bronco rider.

I held on for dear life as we sped towards daylight, the sides of the tunnel passing in a blur of greens and yellows. I was starting to tire and felt my hold on the crocodile's back slipping. But I knew that if I let go I would be instant fast-food. I had to do something.

Reaching over my shoulder with one hand, I felt around in my rucksack until I found the ball of string I had packed as part of my explorer's kit. Gripping the crocodile with my legs, I managed to make a slipknot at one end of the string. Then, ever so slowly, I edged my way up its long slippery back, pushing myself forward until I was astride its head.

This was it. I knew I only had one chance. Any slip-up and I would drop straight into the croc's deadly jaws. As we raced out of the tunnel into dazzling sunlight, I lunged forward and passed the loop of the string around its snout and pulled with all my might. The knot slipped up the string and drew the loop tight around the croc's jaws. Now it couldn't bite and all I had to do was wait for it to tire.

I was still congratulating myself when we shot straight out into mid-air, like a bullet from a gun. The river had come to a sudden halt in a high, roaring waterfall!

Far From Home

Down, down I dropped, still astride the crocodile's back.

Through billows of spray and down through the coloured arc of a rainbow, until *THWACK!* we hit the water and I was knocked clear of the reptile and sank in a roar of foam.

Buffeted and battered like a rag in a washing machine, I kicked for the surface, praying that my loop of string would hold tight around the crocodile's snout.

I broke through the surface, and looked desperately around until I spotted the great beast. It was floating stunned and winded on the other side of the wide lake that pooled at the base of the falls. The string was still tied firmly around its mouth.

I swam for the shore and clambered out, shaking with exhaustion, and carefully edged near to where the crocodile flopped pathetically in the shallows. Then, quick as I could, I yanked at the string and freed the croc from its muzzle.

It drifted away, tired and defeated.

Panting, I reached round to put the ball of string back in my rucksack. My hand brushed against something sharp. It was one of the crocodile's teeth wedged into the buckle! I pulled it out. The tooth was razor sharp, serrated like a steak knife and as big as my hand. Fantastic!

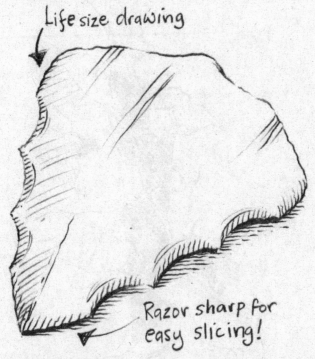

Life size drawing

Razor sharp for easy slicing!

I wrapped the tooth in some leaves and pushed it right to the bottom of my rucksack. I couldn't wait to show everyone at school. It

was undeniable proof that I'd wrestled a croc
and lived to tell the tale!

But then, as I looked around to get my
bearings, I began to wonder if I'd ever be going
to school again. Because I could see
immediately that absolutely EVERYTHING
had changed!

The waterfall had tumbled me down over three hundred metres of sheer cliff, and there was no way I could climb back up. And I couldn't see any paths leading away from the lake either. It was surrounded by trees that grew in a tangle right up to the water's edge. Trees so tall and thick and vine-covered that they looked suspiciously like a jungle. A dark, steamy jungle!

As the air echoed to the sounds of unfamiliar birds and animals, I wondered if I had dropped into some sort of incredible theme park. But that was crazy. I was pretty sure I'd have heard if a new one was going to open anywhere near my house. So where on earth was I?

I was in a tight spot, that's where I was!

I looked back up the huge cliff-face and decided I should probably let Mum know that I might be a bit late for tea. Rummaging in my rucksack, I found my mobile and dialled. Amazingly I managed to get a signal.

'Mum!' I cried when she answered the phone.

'Oh, hello, darling, is everything all right?'

'Yeah, it's brilliant! But Mum, I've discovered

this weird river and I seem to have toppled over a waterfall into a deep valley.'

'Sounds wonderful, dear,' she replied. 'Oh, wait a minute, Charlie. Here's your dad just come in. Now remember, don't be late for tea, and if you're passing the shops on the way back, please pick up a pint of milk. Bye.'

'Hold on a minute, Mum—' I began. But she had already hung up.

Never mind, I thought, returning my phone to the bottom of my bag. I could tell her everything when I got home. I eyed the heavy undergrowth. Whenever that might be.

Into The Jungle

I set off through the tangle of trees and bushes and was soon covered in scratches and bruises. My trainers were full of mud and water, but I didn't care. What are a few scratches to a bold adventurer? Would Neil Armstrong have abandoned his moon mission just because he'd scuffed his best shoes? I don't think so!

I pushed bravely onwards, keeping my eyes peeled all the time. The jungle air was filled with the sounds of strange beasts, and after my encounter with the crocodile I knew I had to tread really carefully.

Calls drifted down from the treetops, and I could hear growls, grunts and snuffles as mysterious creatures scrambled through the undergrowth. But although I heard the rustle of leaves overhead, and the cracking of twigs on the ground, I didn't see anything at all – just endless trees and bushes. And every time I bent back a branch, or pushed nervously through some vines, I thought I might come face to face with something horrible!

But it wasn't possible to stay scared for too long, because everything in this strange new world was so wonderful. The trees were draped with lichen-covered creepers and strange fruits hung in great clusters from their branches. Some of the leaves were as large as tablecloths and as tough as leather.

One fell to the ground just as I was passing through a small clearing and I decided it would make another great trophy to show off at school. I rolled it up, and was just adding it to my explorer's kit when I had the strangest feeling that I was being watched.

I darted a look around the clearing, but I

could see nothing. Just more trees!

Feeling uneasy, I slipped back into the undergrowth and pressed on as quickly as I dared. I was sure that I could hear the rustle of leaves and the careful tread of footsteps behind me. But every time I stopped, so did the footsteps, and every time I started off, there they were again.

It was not a nice feeling! I didn't like it at all. And my imagination started going into overdrive. What could it be? A man-eating tiger perhaps? Or a sly and hungry wolf? Or maybe it was someone from home, my dad or a friend looking for me. There was only one way to find out. I took a deep breath and swung round suddenly.

There, just a few metres back, amongst the dark leaves, was a pair of angry red eyes, staring right at me.

I ran!

I ran as fast as I could through the tangle of branches, aware of the footsteps behind getting closer and closer. Then, all of a sudden, the jungle stopped and I raced out into a vast clearing – a plain of yellow grassland that stretched all the way to the horizon.

A pair of angry red
eyes were staring
at me...

Whatever it was that had been following me
stayed hidden in the trees, and I knew that I
was safe. 'Phew!' I gasped in relief. 'That was
close!'

But as I stared across the empty savannah, I
felt cold inside. I'd half-convinced myself that
when the jungle ended, I'd find myself not too
far from town. Perhaps just on the other side
of the ring-road. But now, faced with
grasslands almost as far as the eye could see, I
was almost certain that I wouldn't be back
home in time for tea.

'This is going to take some explaining!' I muttered, reaching for my phone again.

I was just about to dial the number when the ground started to rumble and shake. A terrific noise like an express train filled the air. I looked up and dropped my phone in fright. Charging at full speed towards me was a rampaging rhinoceros!

All Steamed Up

I stood rooted to the spot as, head down, the rhino charged. His nostrils were spouting great clouds of steam that swirled around his body, so it seemed as if he was on fire. His skin was puckered and covered in a great eruption of boils, and his legs pumped back and forth with a thumping and swishing that sounded like huge pistons. Closer and closer the huffing, snorting beast stampeded. His horn, shining like polished silver, was pointing straight at me!

'STOP!' I managed to squeak, squeezing my eyes tight shut. And at that precise moment, with an explosion of steam, the rhinoceros ground to a halt just centimetres away.

I opened my eyes, hardly daring to breathe,

The rhinoceros ground to a halt.

and waved away the fog of steam that coiled
around me. The rhino stared back, nostrils
bubbling like a boiling kettle, but didn't move.
Slowly I raised my arm and touched him on the
nose. He was made of tin! I tapped him harder,
but still he didn't move. No matter how hard I
rapped and banged he stayed as still as a statue!

Carefully I circled the rhinoceros, all
thoughts of phoning home forgotten. His body
was a series of shaped and scalloped sheets of
armour plating, fastened together with heavy

bolts. What I had thought were boils were really great domed rivets as large as ping-pong balls. His neck and legs were made of chain-mail, allowing them to move and bend, and his tail was formed from a series of interlocking joints ending in a large, diamond-shaped club. I'd never seen or heard of anything like him. Was he a beast or a machine? Whichever he was, he was absolutely magnificent.

Completing a circuit of this remarkable beast, I was amazed to find what looked like a hatchway in his side. I gave the rhino another pat, just to make sure he wasn't going to spring back into life, and his great body echoed like an empty oil drum. Then, using the screwdriver tool on my penknife, I unscrewed the bolts that held the hatch door in place. It opened with a rusty screech and I peered inside.

As a cloud of steam dispersed, I could see a mass of pipes and dials. The rhino was a machine! A very complicated and sophisticated one.

The pipes twisted and turned like metallic intestines, joining, separating and diverting from one another on their convoluted route inside the great barrel of the rhino's belly. At their centre was a water tank, and on it was riveted an oval badge, which read: 'Jakeman's Works. The Steam-Powered Rhinoceros. Patent No. 102633.' *Brilliant*, I thought. *Steam powered!*

Peering more closely to try to see how the rhino might work, I saw a slip of paper lodged in a spring clip on the inside of his belly-plate. Here's what it looked like...

(I'll stick it in the next page of this journal so you can see how incredible it is too!)

I studied the diagram for a few minutes, and then leaned inside the rhino again. A small pilot-light underneath the water tank was popping and flickering, but when I unscrewed the cap on the tank itself, I could see it was completely dry. Fetching the water bottle from my rucksack, I carefully filled the tank up. The main dial had flipped to ROARING HOT, which I guessed might have accounted for the rhino's fiery disposition, so I turned the pointer down to COOL. Then I pressed RESET on the main panel, and sat back to see what would happen to this very, very rare steam-powered beast.

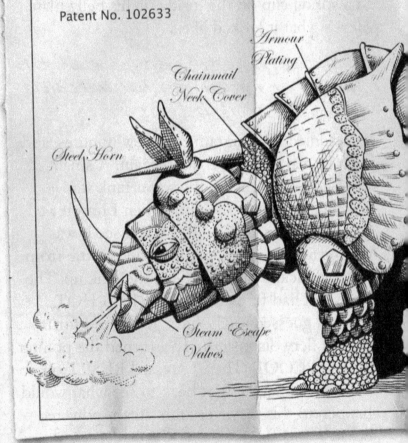

Jakeman's Patented
Steam Powered Rhinoceros

Patent No. 102633

Armour Plating

Chainmail Neck Cover

Steel Horn

Steam Escape Valves

Control
Panel

Insulated Saddle

Hatch To
Controls

Water Tank

Articulated
Tail

Iron
Scales

Chainmail

Riding The Rhino

The pilot-light fired the rhino's burners and the water started to heat up. Soon it was bubbling merrily and, as the steam went coursing through his pipes and valves, the rhino turned his head and looked at me.

'Good boy, good rhino,' I said a bit nervously, patting his snout as he nudged me gently with his great head. Then, with a squirt of steam, the rhino harrumphed, dipped his head and started to tug and chew at the dry grasses, taking on fuel for his internal furnace. It was amazing! And the inventor had to be some kind of genius. So long as there was food and water around, this mechanical rhino could keep going for ever. But what was it doing out here, on the sun-drenched savannah?

As I rubbed behind his ears, the rhino closed his eyes in ecstasy. 'That's it, stay cool, Rhino,' I said calmly. Then I had a great idea. Maybe the rhino could help me cross the plain and find a pathway home. After all, there was no going back the way I had come.

Reaching into my rucksack, I pulled out the

ball of string. Cutting off a length, I looped it through the rhino's mouth to act as reins, and cautiously climbed onto his back.

'OK,' I said, giving him a gentle kick, 'let's go!'

With a few metallic squeaks and squeals, the rhinoceros lumbered into motion and trotted across the plain.

'Faster,' I cried, flicking the reins. 'Faster!'

The rhino broke into a canter, and we tore through the tall grasses and headed towards a distant green smudge that I thought might be more forest. I'd not even ridden a horse before, but here I was on the back of a huge metal rhino, screaming across a sun-drenched plain that glowed in the late afternoon sun. The grasses swayed in the slight breeze, creating wave after wave that rippled across the savannah, making it look like a golden ocean. My rhino putt-putted across this sea like a little steamboat, leaving a trail of flattened grass in our wake. I stood up in the saddle, imagining

how easy it would be to herd cattle with such a powerful steed.

'Yee-hah!' I whooped.

But after hours of lumbering forwards I started to feel a bit disheartened. The plain truly was vast, and the forest just wasn't getting any closer. I was starting to wish I'd had a bit more riding experience, too – bouncing up and down in the metal saddle was becoming a real pain in the bum. Every juddering, jolting stride the rhino took rattled my bones and bruised my behind!

I'd been worried about missing tea, but now I didn't think I'd even make it home before dark. It looked like I was going to have to camp out for the night in an unknown land, under a strange sky. Just like a real explorer. The thought made me feel a whole lot better. Until I remembered Mum. And imagined the look on her face when I told her I was planning to camp out – without a tent! Sighing, I reached for my mobile again . . .

Very Late For Tea

I couldn't get a signal on my phone, but a few

miles away I could see a lone palm tree climbing tall and straight from the middle of the plain. Maybe if I shinned up its trunk I could get a better signal, I thought. I turned the rhino towards it.

But my plan was foiled. As we got closer, I could see that the trunk of the huge palm was as smooth as glass and impossible to climb. I slid down from the rhino's back and sank into the tall grasses that waved above my head. I suddenly felt very lonely, stuck in the middle of this endless plain, in a strange land and with the sun starting to go down.

There was nothing I could do but make camp for the night. I would have to phone Mum tomorrow, as soon as I could get a signal. But, as I waded through the grasses, trying to flatten them into a bed, I tripped. Looking down, I saw a thin silver thread stretched between the stalks. Surely I couldn't have tripped over that, I thought. Grabbing the strand, I tried to snap it in half, but I couldn't. It was incredibly strong.

Curious, I followed the thread through the grasses until it joined another thread, then another, and another, until my finger had traced its way to the centre of a huge, complicated spider's web. A shiny, electric-blue spider, about the size of a walnut, came out to see what it had caught and sat staring at me from halfway up a grass stalk. Not more spider's webs, I thought.

Feeling slightly shaken, I stood back and inspected the gem-bright creature. It didn't seem worried that I had trampled through its home, and immediately started to make repairs.

Electric blue
Spider.

Really
strong
thread.

Whirring like a clockwork toy, the spider quickly spun metres of extra-strong thread. And as I sat watching the industrious little creature, I had an idea. It might be able to help me phone home!

Plucking the spider from its web, I placed it on its back in the palm of my hand. A strand of silk thread poked from the tip of its abdomen. I pulled the thread gently, and a little more appeared. I tugged again, and more thread spooled into my hand. It was just like unravelling a cotton reel! I tested the strength of the thread once more and then tied the end to my right index finger. Then I took the spider in my right hand and threw it high into the air with all my might. Up it flew – five metres, ten metres, fifteen – right over the top of the palm tree!

The spider arced through the air, spinning out a length of silky yarn all the way, until it fell unharmed into the grass on the far side. I untied the thread from my finger, tied it firmly to the rhino's horn, and then rushed to find the spider amongst the tangle of grasses.

Following the thread as it zigzagged amongst the tall stems, I quickly caught up with the little blue web-maker. And, before it had a chance to scuttle away, I bent down and snipped the thread from its abdomen with my penknife. Then, careful not to get myself tangled in the long sticky strand, I tied the end to the belt tab of my jeans. The spider-line was now in a great loose loop that went from my belt, way up over the tree, and down the other side to the rhino, and I was ready to put my idea into action.

'Walk on, Rhino, walk on!' I cried, slapping his tin flank with my palm. The friendly steam-powered rhinoceros lumbered slowly away, taking up the slack, and as the thread tightened, I was lifted off the ground!

Once I'd reached the top of the tree, I hastily pulled the phone from my pocket.

Rhino.

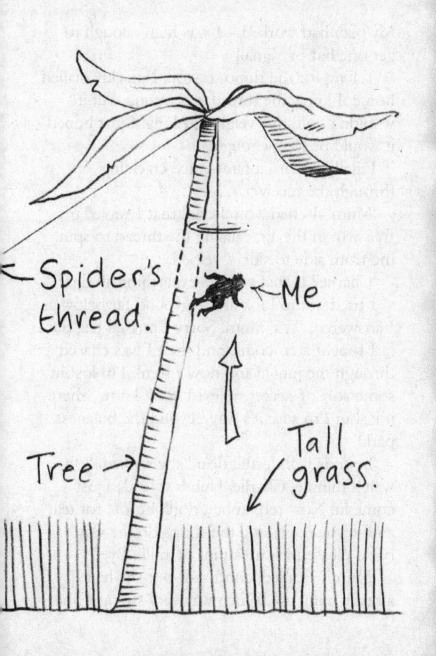

Spider's thread.

Me

Tree →

Tall grass.

My plan had worked – I was high enough to get one bar of signal!

Yelling for the rhino to stop, I quickly dialled home. I knew the thread was strong, but it wouldn't hold my weight for long. I just hoped it would be long enough.

Finally I heard a faint voice crackling through the receiver.

'Mum!' I cried, so relieved that I waved my free arm in the air, causing the thread to spin me from side to side. I yelped.

'Charlie? Is that you? Is everything all right?'

I tried not to look at the ground far below as I answered, 'Yes, Mum. Sorry I missed tea, but . . . I fought a crocodile and then I was chased through the jungle and now I think I'm lost in some sort of secret valley! I don't know where it is, but I'm sure it's way beyond the business park!'

'Sounds wonderful, dear,' she replied. 'Oh, wait a minute, Charlie. Here's your dad just come in. Now remember, don't be late for tea, and if you're passing the shops on the way back, please pick up a pint of milk. Bye.'

'Mum?' I called, confused. But she had already hung up. Which was very strange! She hadn't seemed worried at all. In fact, she'd said the exact same things as when I'd phoned from the river, hours and hours ago. It was as if she hadn't heard a word I'd said. As if no time had passed at all.

Where was I? Had the waterfall swept me into another part of the world? Had I found some sort of lost kingdom just round the corner from home? Or maybe I'd been blasted into a different time dimension by the lightning strike! They were all pretty scary thoughts, but at least I knew I hadn't missed tea yet.

A sudden gust of wind sent me spinning again, and I decided I'd better not waste any more time thinking until I was safely back on the ground. I called out to the steam-powered rhino, and as he backed up I was gently lowered down into the grass.

My First Night Under The Stars

The sky has turned black and is glittering with stars, and I've just finished making camp. There are no boulders out here to shelter behind, and the palm tree is too tall and bendy to make a bed in, so I'm having to sleep down in the grass.

By leading the rhino round and round in ever-increasing circles, I at least got the stalks stomped down enough to make a flattish patch to lie on. It's sheltered from the wind, but now that the sun has gone down, it's really cold.

For a while I thought I might have to put my coat back on over my pyjamas, but as I was trying to get comfortable on the stubbled and prickly ground, the rhino stepped over and is now sheltering me beneath his bulging stomach. The heat from his furnace is making my grassy bed cosy and warm, and by opening the hatch in his side, I've enough light to write by.

But even now I've written down everything that's happened so far, I still can't make head or tail of it.

What exactly happened to bring me to this amazing place? Why, for Mum, is it still only nearly teatime, when for me it's way past midnight? At least I don't have to worry about her worrying about me. She has no idea what's been happening to me!

Wow! I've just realized . . . if Mum isn't missing me, then no one will come looking for me. I'm going to have to rely on myself. This is for real! I'm actually in the great adventure I always dreamed of!

Wherever this place is, whether I'm the first explorer to ever set foot in it or not I may never know. But as long as I'm here, I'm going to try to behave like a real explorer. I'm going to make as many entries in this journal as I can, and collect lots of evidence to prove it's all true.

Laughter In The Night

Wow – how lucky was I to have made a friend of the metal rhino! In the middle of the night I woke up as a peal of laughter rang through the darkness. Who could it be? I wondered, my heart starting to pound.

I sat up quickly, banging my head on the rhino's belly and making it ring like a bell. The laughter stopped instantly, but as I peered across our makeshift campsite, I could see the grasses swaying and jerking to the movements of uninvited guests. Then the stalks stopped moving and the clang from the rhino faded into a tense silence. I waited.

As my eyes grew accustomed to the dark, I could make out vague shapes in the grass. They

slunk and slithered and crept around the
perimeter of the camp, and I thought I could
hear empty bellies rumbling with hunger. Then
their low chuckles and sniggers rose again from
all around the camp, and a burst of manic
laughter echoed across the night sky.
Suddenly I knew: hyenas!

But why weren't they attacking?

Hee Hee

Ha Ha Ha!

I decided they must be wary of my metallic friend, the steam-powered rhinoceros. They hadn't yet worked out that his repetitive gurgles and hisses were a sign that he was deep in mechanical slumber. I turned quickly to rap on his tummy, but at that moment one particularly brave animal broke cover and made a dash for me.

Before I could do anything about it, the hyena's jaws were clamped firmly around my ankle and I was being dragged from underneath the rhino! Saliva was drooling from the hungry beast's mouth, and I could feel its sticky warmth seeping into my sock as its teeth dug into the thick rubber sole of my trainer.

'Help!' I yelled.

The hyena began pulling me towards the wall of grasses, and I knew that the minute I disappeared amongst those tall, densely packed stems, I would be lost for ever.

I yelled and squirmed and kicked at the hyena's wide, bony head, but its mighty jaws gripped even tighter.

It was at this precise moment that I remembered reading something about hyenas on one of my wild animal collector's cards, and now that I'm writing up this adventure, from the safety of a jungle tree, I will stick the card in my book:

PREDATOR RATING 10

THE HYENA

Hyenas are scavengers by day but ferocious killers at night. They have the most powerful jaws in the whole of the animal kingdom, even stronger than the great white shark's. This allows them to snap the very largest of bones like twigs. Hyenas can digest the flesh, bones, fur, feathers, horns and teeth of their prey. There is never anything left. Remember, if a hyena carries its tail out straight, it is a signal that it is about to attack.

WILD ANIMAL COLLECTORS CARDS

Interesting facts, certainly. Interesting, but not very useful when your foot is stuck in a hyena's mouth! My bones felt as if they were about to shatter like a sheet of glass and I screamed again.

The rhino woke up suddenly, exhaling a great spout of steam. And, with a huge bellow, he charged. Immediately the hyena let me go. Snarling and drooling, it turned to face the attack. But it didn't stand a chance against the power of the rhinoceros, and the fight was over in an instant. Hooking his metal horn under the scavenger's belly, the rhino sent it sailing through the air and off into the darkness.

Moments later there was a dull thud, and a plaintive yelp. The rhino let out another huge hiss of steam, trotted back into the campsite, closed his eyes and went straight back to sleep. What a hero!

I scuttled back under his belly, but I didn't find it as easy to get to sleep as my metal friend. The hyenas didn't try another raid, but they circled the camp for the rest of the night, and every time I closed my eyes I imagined my bones being crunched by ravenous predators.

My bones crunched to powder!

A Charliesmallicus

Things looked better in the morning, despite my ankle feeling sore and bruised. Even though I only had grass shoots and a solitary mint for breakfast. (I wanted to scoff the lot, but I knew the packet might have to last me a very long time!)

I climbed onto the rhino's back and we set off for the line of trees that stretched across the horizon. I patted his neck and the rhino let out a joyful jet of steam. He was a good companion to have.

My first breakfast!

The air smelled clean and fresh, the sun was warm on my back, and the plain was alive with creatures both familiar and strange. I saw elephants and panthers, highly coloured paradise birds and, when we stopped for a drink at a watering hole, I could still hear the hyenas howling in the distance.

A Paradise
Bird.

But I also saw a strange, weird and exotic animal that I'm pretty sure has never been seen by humans before – or since!

I know from my books at home that if an explorer discovers an unrecorded species, they should describe and name the creature. So I've decided to do the same.

Here is the first of my discoveries. The size of a cat, it broke cover from the grass whilst I sat at the watering hole, watching the animals and enjoying the sun. With a piercing 'PEEP!' it jumped over my outstretched legs, grabbed a melon-sized fruit from the trunk of a grazing elephant, and disappeared into the grasses again!

The Charliesmallicus

(Sketched from memory.)

Fast, fearless and intelligent. (All good explorers name at least one thing after themselves!)

The steam-powered rhino sucked up gallons of extra water into his tank at the watering hole, and munched down armfuls of dry grass for fuel. As I called him over in readiness to continue our journey, he harrumphed in a way that seemed to say that he was ready for anything.

Although he couldn't speak, I found his presence very comforting. He had already proved a good friend and a formidable ally, and I felt that I could rely on him entirely. I knew that if it hadn't been for him, I would be nothing more than a slight case of indigestion for a rather fat hyena!

As I gathered my bits and pieces from the ground, he lumbered up behind me and gently rested his great head on my shoulder.

'Good boy,' I said, patting his snout as he

hissed with contentment. 'Time to get going.' I picked up my rucksack and climbed onto the rhino's broad back.

Whatever this land was called, I had arrived at a truly incredible place. As the rhino carried me across the golden plain, with the sun shining and animals calling, I tingled with excitement. I felt invincible, ready to tackle anything. And there, at last, was the jungle, less than a mile away and glittering dark green in the sunlight.

'Come on, Rhino,' I called, giving him a kick to hurry him along. 'Nearly there!'

We galloped full pelt down a gentle slope towards the first fringe of trees. Now I felt we were getting somewhere. With any luck the rhino could plough straight through the jungle like a bulldozer. When I got to the other side, I might find a path that would lead me back home.

Nothing could go wrong now.

But then the grasses in front of us began to rustle like crackling flames. Something was lurking within them. Something huge!

The grasses waved frantically back and forth and, suddenly, rising like a monster from the depths, a massive snake was towering over us!

Snake Bite

The serpent glowed, iridescent in the sunlight.
Colours pulsed across its skin like electricity:
purples and greens and yellows. The snake's
body was as thick as a car's tyre, its head as
large as a stallion's. The steam-powered rhino
stopped in his tracks and grunted, hunching his
back and pawing the ground with his foreleg.
Carefully the snake and the rhino circled each
other, waiting for the right moment to strike. I
had the distinct impression that these two
animals had met before and had unfinished
business to attend to.

I decided that I definitely didn't want to be
stuck on the rhino's back while the two giant
beasts fought, and I started looking frantically
around for a hiding place. But I was too late.
The serpent, hissing like the air brakes of a
huge lorry, spotted me on the rhino's back and
started coiling and writhing in ecstasy. It had
clearly decided that I was some kind of rare
treat, and was determined not to miss this
opportunity to have a bite.

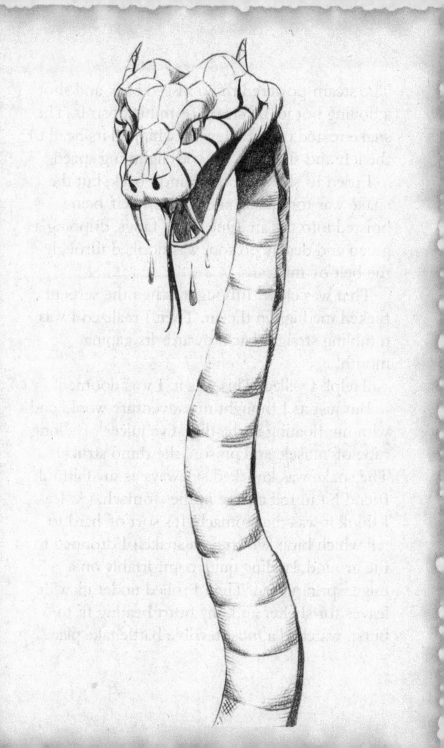

The steam-powered rhino hissed back and shot a boiling hot jet of steam from his nostrils. The snake reared out of the way, whipped its head to the left and struck at me with lightning speed.

I tried to slip from the rhino's back, but the snake was too quick, and I felt myself being hoisted into the air. One of its fangs, dripping a green and deadly poison, was hooked through the belt of my jeans.

That was close! I thought, when the serpent flicked me high in the air. Then I realized I was tumbling straight back towards its gaping mouth!

'Help!' I yelled. This was it. I was doomed!

But just as I thought my adventure would end with me floating in the digestive juices of a long tube of muscle and poison, the rhino struck! The snake was knocked sideways as my faithful friend hit it, full charge in the stomach. (At least, I think it was the stomach. It's sort of hard to tell which bit is which on a snake!) I dropped to the ground, landing quite comfortably on a huge, springy fern. Then I rolled under its wide leaves for shelter and, my heart beating fit to burst, watched a most terrible battle take place.

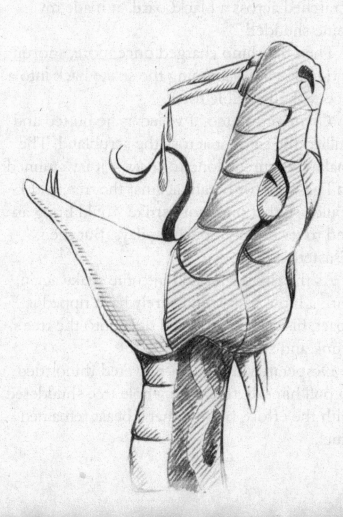

A Fight To The Death!

The snake fought back, but its fangs scraped
uselessly against the rhino's metal sides. The
sound was like the screech of fingernails being
scratched across a blackboard. It made my
spine shudder!

Then the rhino charged once more, snorting
and bellowing, slamming the snake back into a
tree with incredible force.

'Come on, Rhino,' I yelled as he butted and
bullied the serpent across the scrubland. The
snake was surely done for now – it lay stunned
and gasping for breath against the tree, and I
could see that one more strike would bring an
end to its rhino-ambushing days. But then,
disaster!

As the rhino smashed into the snake again,
with a blow that would surely have ripped it
apart, his steel horn sliced deep into the tree's
trunk and stuck fast.

Desperately the steam-powered rhino tried
to pull himself free. The whole tree shuddered
with the effort, but the metal beast remained
stuck.

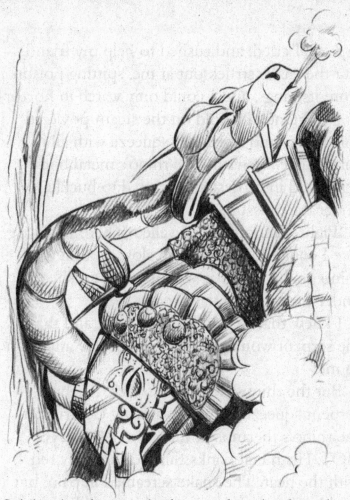

Seizing its chance, the battered snake darted under the rhino's stomach and up over his back, quickly encircling him in coil after glistening coil of rippling, muscled body. With one huge effort, the rhino ripped his horn from the tree, but it was all too late.

'No!' I cried, and rushed to help my friend. But the snake struck out at me, spitting poison from its fangs, and I could only watch in horror as it tightened its hold on the steam-powered rhinoceros and started to squeeze with all its formidable strength. The rhino's metal body screeched in protest as it started to buckle under the pressure.

'Fight, Rhino, fight!' I yelled. There was little else I could do, and as if in slow motion the rhino gradually collapsed, his sides crushed under the snake's mighty coils.

I knew that he had lost the battle and that the serpent would then turn its deadly attention to me.

But the rhino had one last trick. As the serpent squeezed him like a living car-crusher, the rhino's thermostat flicked to BOILING HOT. His metal flanks flushed suddenly red with the heat. The snake screamed in pain, but couldn't let go. It knew the rhino still had enough strength to lunge with his deadly horn.

So the snake gripped, and the rhino grew hotter and hotter, his sides glowing like a hot plate, searing the snake to his metal skin like a rasher of bacon to a frying pan.

The snake, smoking and cooked to a turn, gasped its last breath. But the poor old rhino's workings had gone beyond the point of no return. With a terrible shudder the poor crushed animal exploded!

I dived back under the fern as bits of metal piping and lumps of snake rained down. Then a large glass marble dropped from the sky and rolled in front of me. I turned it over and saw that it was one of the steam-powered rhino's glass eyes. I bit my lip to keep my eyes from watering as I put it in my bag. It was a terrible end to my adventure with such a brave and incredible creature, but at least I had something to remember him by – and proof that he was real!

Bits of metal continued to fall and the ground was soon covered in shards of red-hot shrapnel. Suddenly, *PUFF!* The dry grass burst into flame and a wall of fire raced across the ground

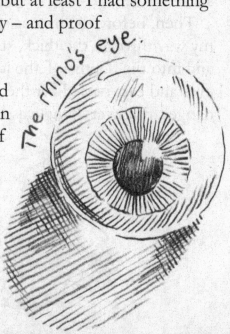

The rhino's eye.

at an alarming speed. Grabbing a slab of well-cooked snake, I ran for the jungle before the fire could cut off my escape route.

Smashing into the trees, I turned to look back at the scene of devastation I had just escaped. My poor friend the rhino littered the ground in a hundred different parts, and the pack of manic hyenas that had been following us all day was slinking between the fires and piles of smoking metal. Snarling and quarrelling, they fell hungrily on the snake meat that littered the ground. It reminded me of how hungry I was, and I ravenously bit into my snake burger.

Then, before the hyenas spotted me, I forced my way through the thick, strong undergrowth and into the depths of the jungle. I kept my eyes and ears peeled for the signs of any new danger. But everything was strangely quiet.

My First Night In The Jungle

Trees of every shade of green soared above me. Thick and limbless, their trunks shot way up into the murky height of the forest canopy. Wherever I could, I followed animal paths through the dense undergrowth, and if my way was barred, I hacked at the ferns and creepers with my penknife.

Every now and then the cry of a distant animal or the nearby rustling of leaves broke the eerie silence of the jungle. It gave me the jitters. I couldn't help remembering the scary red eyes I'd seen on the other side of the vast plain, and I wished the steam-powered rhino was still at my side.

Coming to a clearing, I stopped in my tracks. For here was a wide, clear pool, fed by a babbling stream that looked exactly like the one at the bottom of my garden! It had the same tinkling sound and the same moss-covered, stony bottom. Could it somehow be the same stream? I wondered. Was I really just a stone's throw from my own back door after all? Maybe my garden was just the other side of the tangle of bushes – like a portal in a sci-fi story.

I ran, my heart beating fast.

'Made it!' I yelled at the top of my voice, crashing through the foliage. 'Home at last!'

But I was answered only by the cries of a band of scarlet parrots that darted through the leaves overhead. It was not a magical doorway to home. I was still inside the jungle. A jungle that could be anywhere in the world . . . or beyond.

Suddenly I felt very tired and flopped down on the bank of the stream. I undid my water bottle and pushed it below the surface, letting it fill to the brim. I held the bottle up to what light there was to check for anything horrible wriggling about, then took gulp after gulp of the cool, clear water. Then I started to look for somewhere to spend the night.

I decided I'd be safer up a tree, away from any nocturnal beasts that might be roaming the forest floor, so I picked up my rucksack and started to climb one of the giant trunks.

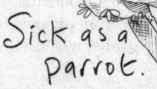

Sick as a parrot.

The rough bark made it an easy climb and I quickly reached a huge branch that grew out across the jungle floor thirty metres below. The branch was so wide it was easy to walk along, and near the end I discovered a very handy platform, covered in grass and leaves. It was almost as if someone had made it specially.

Now I'm snuggled down in the thick, musty covering and trying to write down everything that's happened. This is the second night I've not made it home in time for tea, and I wonder how many more nights I'll have to camp out under the stars. Not that I care! I'm having

the adventure of a lifetime in this mysterious
land and I feel safe and snug in this jungle nest.
But I'm really tired after everything that's
happened. I can hardly keep my eyes open.

I must . . . get . . . some . . . sleep.

*If I had known that
something was watching me
from up in the forest canopy,
I wouldn't have fallen asleep so easily!*

The Roof ~~Of~~ Of The Jungle

Waking up early the next morning, I lay sleepily
watching a strange and beautiful humming
moth. It was hovering by the large purple
flowers that grew on the vines hanging from
the trees all around me. It was drinking the
nectar through a tongue that was as long as a
shoelace!

The moth flitted from one flower to the next
as I folded away my pyjamas, struggled into my
clothes and shrugged my rucksack onto my
back. It was such a beautiful sight that I began

to wonder why I'd been so nervous of the jungle the night before.

Then a huge and hairy hand reached down out of the mass of leaves above me, and I was hoisted up through the air!

I found myself staring into the dark and angry red eyes that I had seen in the jungle on my first day. They belonged to a colossal silverback gorilla!

With a grunt, he gripped me between his feet and, using his powerful arms, swung off through the trees.

'Help,' I cried, staring down at the jungle floor passing in a wild blur far below.

'Stop!' I beat on his ankles and tugged at his coarse black hair, but I don't think the gorilla felt a thing.

Surely I wasn't going to be his breakfast? After escaping the crocodile, the hyenas and the serpent, it all seemed rather unfair. What was it with this place that everything tried to eat you? But as I was soon to find out, breakfast was not what the gorilla had in mind at all!

For hour after hour we swung through the trees, the gorilla never tiring, his pace never slowing. I started to feel terribly travel sick with the constant, stomach-churning swinging and the blur of leaves flashing past my face. Then the silverback started to climb up through the branches, higher and higher. Vague images whizzed past my eyes: glowering faces, grimacing, canine-toothed mouths; until, when it seemed we could go no higher, the silverback came to a halt.

We had arrived at our destination: an incredible gorilla city in the sky!

All around us stretched an immense and

complicated network of platforms. They were built into the very tops of the jungle trees, and then down through the foliage for half a dozen levels, all connected by walkways and bridges and vines.

Although my vision was a bit blurred from the bumpy ride, I could see that each platform was made of planks of wood and bark, all bound together with creepers. The planks were rough and looked as if they had been torn from the sides of a tree by brute force. Some of the platforms had fences around their edges; others were covered by rickety shelters, with walls made from woven fronds.

Moving between platforms, lazing on branches or busy grooming a friend was a whole colony of gorillas! They swung through the trees on hanging creepers, some nursing babies in their arms, others stopping atop a platform for a chat with another gorilla, or to pick up some fruit and continue on their way as if they were strolling through a shopping mall.

Everywhere gorillas were going about their daily business, but as soon as they saw us they started to whoop and scream and chatter. The big silverback climbed to the very highest platform and dropped me in a heap.

I lay in a daze as the big ape thumped his mighty chest like a big bass drum and called the gorillas to order.

The tribe gathered around as he spoke to them with a series of grimaces and grunts. I couldn't understand what was going on, but the silverback seemed very pleased that he had captured me. He poked me in the tummy, sat me down, stood me up and pushed me with his thick, leathery forefinger, making me take a few wobbly steps. Feeling very woozy, I couldn't offer any resistance.

The gorillas chattered in delight, but when one of the others tried to pick me up, the silverback roared a warning, his lips folded back to reveal a row of impressive teeth.

The other gorillas backed away and watched from a distance as the silverback played with me like a rag doll, and I suddenly realized that this was exactly how he thought of me! As some sort of doll! I was the gorilla equivalent of a cuddly toy!

How embarrassing!

I looked around to see if there was any chance of escape, but it was impossible. We were high in the canopy of the jungle, and the gorillas were so skilled at moving through the trees that they would be on me before I could climb a fraction of the way to the ground. I decided I would have to bide my time and wait to see what happened next.

The Gorilla's Pet

Things just go from bad to worse! Now I'm locked in a cage. Silverback has made it from twigs as strong and flexible as whips. It hangs above his platform and I'm placed here every night, or when he goes off on one of his hunting trips. I don't mind too much about that part, though. I'm so grateful to have a break from him that I haven't even bothered to try

and escape yet. Instead, if I've not been keeping the horrible silverback amused, I've just snoozed the days away in this cage. But now I think it's time to bring my journal up to date.

Promise me one thing. If you ever have a pet puppy or budgie, PLEASE don't make it do tricks. Don't make it beg or roll over, and don't teach it to talk. Just let it behave like a little dog or bird. I know how humiliating it is to be made to do silly tricks day after day! The silverback pokes and prods me, making me walk one way then the other, back and forth, back and forth until I scream with boredom. And this delights him even more! He loves to hear me shout at him. 'Leave me alone, you big, hairy lummox,' I yell. But of course he doesn't understand a word. He just grins his foolish grin, pokes me in the back and starts me walking again.

I've lost all track of time. I don't know if it's Tuesday or Wednesday, or if I've been in this jungle for two days or two weeks. All I can tell is if it's day or night. At the moment it's night-time, and the gorilla's city is lit by hundreds of beautiful lanterns. I have no idea where they come from. Surely they can't have electricity here? But I'm too tired to think about it. I am going to get some sleep after a really exhausting day of marching up and down for the gormless gorilla. I'll write some more tomorrow. Today it was sunny.

The Next Day

Not much happened today. Marched up and down. Sat in my cage and watched Silverback snooze, knowing that as soon as he woke up, he would have me performing tricks for him again. Today it was sunny.

The Day After That

At sunrise today, Silverback went off on a hunting trip, leaving me in my cage. Out of sheer boredom I've tried to saw through the twig bars with my penknife, but they are as tough as leather and the blade just isn't big enough. The crocodile's tooth is no good either. The end is sharp enough to poke into the bars, but even when I wiggle it back and forth as hard as I can, the bars just won't splinter.

I must try and get a new knife from somewhere. Today it was sunny.

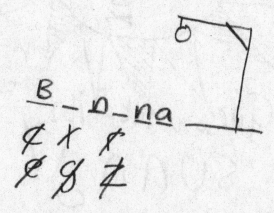

Another Sunny Day

Was made to march up and down for a few hours this morning, then Silverback went out again. Some of the other gorillas have been coming up to my cage, bringing me titbits and trying to talk to me. Of course, I can't understand a word. I think Silverback is on his way back because they've all just scattered. I'd better hide my diary again.

← great hairy twit

Many (Sunny) Days Later

Every time Silverback goes out, the other gorillas come and visit me. By repeating their grunts over and over again, they have managed to teach me a few of their words, and I can now ask for a piece of sugar cane, or a juicy slice of pawpaw as often as I wish!

The pack gorillas are much friendlier than Silverback. He's nothing but a big bully who terrorizes the others to keep his position as leader. I've started to realize that they have just about had enough of him. I wonder if they would ever back me in a showdown with the great silverback dictator?

My daily routine has become so uneventful that I won't bother to add any more to my journal until something EXCITING happens. . .

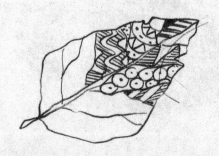

Silverback is a <u>hooligan</u>

I think I'm going Bananas!

↑ the silverback's brain. Actual size.

I am boooored.

I found this ugly looking bug crawling over my notebook. It is highly dangerous. One sting from its tail can make you spontaneously combust. I slammed the book shut on it — sorry about the mess!

SOMETHING EXCITING HAS HAPPENED!

A Challenge

One day Silverback returned to camp from foraging in the jungle, only to find the others had opened my cage and were sat around me, trying to talk with grunts and hand signs. The silverback was not impressed. Screaming maniacally, he charged into the gorilla pack, sending them scurrying out of the way. Then he picked me up and turned to roar at the others. The message was clear: I was his property, so watch it.

But I had had enough. Now was the time to act. Days had gone by and I was bored and missing home. I couldn't stand being the silverback's toy any longer. So when the gorilla put me down and poked me in the back to set me marching once again, I slapped his hand away.

'No!' I yelled, pointing at him. 'I've had enough, do you hear, Mr Big-shot?' I spoke in English, but the meaning was pretty clear. 'I won't be your pet any more. No way, no how!'

The other gorillas screamed in delight, but Silverback let out a roar of indignation and

Thrak challenges me to an arm wrestling contest.

brought his arm crashing down like a sledgehammer. I leaped out of the way as his fist whizzed past my head. It would have cracked like a boiled egg! Again the pack laughed. I thumped my chest and yelled in fear and relief.

With a low growl, the silverback turned to stare at me from under a beetling brow, his angry eyes glowing red. Very quietly he raised his massive arm, bending it at the elbow and opening his leathery hand. I understood immediately. The great ape was challenging me to an arm-wrestling contest! I gulped. How on earth was I going to get out of this one? And what was going to happen to me WHEN I LOST?

Arm-Wrestling A Gorilla

The silverback and I sat in the middle of the main platform of the gorilla city. This, I discovered later, was where all their important celebrations and ceremonies took place. The rest of the group sat around us in a circle, jostling to try and get the best view. An ancient gorilla, his fur a dirty white, shuffled into the centre of the circle dragging a large branch behind him. This he placed between the glowering silverback and myself.

The branch had been carefully chosen, for it curved up at one end, enabling both the gorilla and me to rest our elbows on it, and for our hands to come to the same level. A must if the competition was going to be fair.

Fair? Who was I kidding! I looked at my tormentor. His shoulders and arms were thick with knotted muscle; his fist was the size of my head. I had no chance. No chance at all! Unless I could come up with a cunning plan.

My mind raced as the ceremony commenced. But I couldn't think of a single thing to do.

The ancient white gorilla addressed the crowd with a series of grunts and hand gestures, laying down the rules of the competition. And at that moment I realized something incredible! I could understand him! Well, I could understand some of what he was saying. I had managed to learn more of the gorillas' language in my little conversations than I had thought.

This was one neat trick, and something I knew I would be able to impress my friends with back home. But before I could even think of home, I had to get through my ordeal with the silverback.

Concentrate, Charlie, I thought to myself. Concentrate.

This is what I managed to follow of the old gorilla's announcement: 'Friends, welcome. This is very important occasion. Thrak is leader. His authority challenged by hairless, pink gorilla. Thrak has decided: quarrel to be settled by arm-wrestling competition.'

Of course he has, I thought, my mind still groping for some sort of plan. He's hardly likely to challenge me to a game of chess!

The gorilla continued. 'Winner of competition will be leader of gorillas. Loser will be banished into darkness of jungle for ever. Let the contest begin!'

I swallowed hard when I heard that bit about banishment. I knew that if I were banished into the jungle straight away, I might end up wandering through the trees for the rest of my life. (Which probably wouldn't be very long!)

I really needed to get to know the maze of

paths that wormed their way through the jungle before I set out alone, and that meant befriending some of the gorillas who'd been coming to my cage. I had to think of a way of winning this one-sided wrestling match.

The excited crowd slapped the platform with their palms in a menacing rhythm and Thrak the silverback processed around the stage like a heavyweight boxer. I thought and thought and, as the drumming built to an ear-splitting crescendo, I had the tiniest of ideas. But it would all rely on the greed of my opponent . . .

We approached the log and nervously I rested my arm on a branch as Thrak closed his giant hand around mine. His hot red eyes bored into me as I waited for the signal to start. If my plan was to work, then I had to get the timing exactly right.

Just as the ancient gorilla was about to slap the trunk as a signal to start, I cried, 'Oh! Just a minute,' and reaching down into my rucksack, I pulled out my bag of humbugs. The gorilla looked on suspiciously as I popped one into my mouth.

'Mmmm,' I said. 'Lovely! OK, let's carry on,' and I reached to put the sweets back.

The gorilla grunted and held out his free hand.

'No way,' I protested, putting the mints in my pocket. But the gorilla growled louder and started to squeeze my hand.

'OK, OK,' I said, holding out the bag. 'Help yourself.' Silverback helped himself to two!

As the gorilla sucked his mints, I waited for the delayed reaction. I knew he wouldn't be used to the strength of Paterchak's mint humbugs. And as the tears sprang to his eyes, I said, 'OK, I'm ready.'

The ancient one gave the signal to start; Thrak let out a gasp of surprise as the heat of the mints hit the back of his throat; and I

pushed the gorilla's arm over as easily as a rather weedy flower!

The silverback fanned his mouth, whooping and hollering and stamping his feet. The pack of gorillas cheered and laughed and raised me high in the air in triumph. I had won! I was the new leader of Gorilla City. But as Thrak retreated in embarrassment, he stared at me with such animosity that I knew we would meet again one day. Then, with a crashing of leaves, the silverback was gone.

The Crowning Of A King

The gorillas were delighted to be free from the bullying rule of Thrak. They organized a celebration that went on for many days, often climbing to the highest branches and screaming across the jungle to wherever the big silverback was nursing his pride. They were warning him never to return.

Part of the noisy celebration was my crowning as the new leader of the gorilla clan! We danced while a band of gorillas slapped out rhythms on hollow tree trunks. We feasted on a selection of fresh and sun-dried fruits, especially chosen for their juicy sweetness. Speeches followed the feasting, and then more speeches. They went on and on, and the more I drank of the gorillas' fermented fruit juice, the less I could understand.

Eventually, after the dancing and the banquet and the speeches, a roughly carved wooden chair was lowered onto the ceremonial platform. It was my throne!

The ancient white gorilla led me to the throne as the rest of the pack hummed a strange incantation. The chanting grew louder, and as it reached an ear-splitting crescendo, a cape of leaves bordered with golden flowers was placed around my shoulders. As the old gorilla raised a crown of intricately woven leaves into the air, the chanting stopped. Then, to complete silence, he placed the crown upon my head. As one, the gorillas cheered: 'All hail King Charlie!'

Hail King charlie!

Now, from my high platform in the trees, I can still hear the gorillas whooping with delight. The partying has started all over again, but I've crept away to write down these fantastic events.

Such a lot has happened!

I've become the leader of a city of apes, but have no idea what it means. What does a gorilla chief do? How am I ever going to make a decent ape? I may be OK at climbing trees for an eight-year-old, but when it comes to swinging from branch to branch hundreds of metres above the ground, I'm going to be rubbish!

Back To School

Yes, I've been back to school! But it's been a lot more fun than anything we ever did at St Beckham's!

I don't want to be king of the apes for ever, but I've decided that if I want to find my way through the jungle, I have to get to know and understand it. And the best way to do that is to become more like a gorilla!

So every morning I've been learning how to

talk in the language of the apes. I had a bit of trouble working out that there are over fifty different words for banana, but apart from that, it's really not been so hard to learn.

Here are some important gorilla phrases, in case you ever find yourself in a sticky situation:

Mmwa (with right palm towards chest): Friend.

Mmwa (with right palm away from chest): Deadly enemy.

Cha: Banana.

Woomwawoomwa (with both palms raised and facing away from chest): Calm down, calm down!

Neeeeaaaaghcha! (whilst jumping up and down and banging the ground with your fists): No, I do not want another banana, thank you. I don't care if I never see another banana again!

Breakfast.   Dinner.   Tea.

In the afternoons I join the younger gorillas for lessons on how to swing from branch to branch in the trees. The gorillas call it sky-walking and it's by far the quickest (and coolest!) way to get around.

I've made two close friends while I've been sky-walking: Grip and Grapple. The three of us spend hours swinging through the trees, racing each other and competing to see who can make

Grip learning to sky walk.

the biggest leaps. When we first started I did as much falling as swinging, but after weeks of aching arms and bumped heads, I can now travel through the canopy at incredible speeds.

It's not all fun stuff though. As king of the gorillas I have a lot of responsibilities, too.

One of my duties is to settle any arguments in the camp. I try to do this by avoiding Thrak's old method of resolving everything with a fight to the death! Over time, by using tips picked up from my books about expedition leaders (be fair but firm!), I have become a popular and respected leader.

But soon I'm going to have to break the news to the tribe that I have to leave. I think I'm just about ready to survive on my own. And I'm really starting to miss Mum's cooking. So I've decided to go exploring again tomorrow to see if I can find a route out of the jungle at last.

A Terrifying Encounter!

How I wish that I'd stayed in the safety of the city and not ventured out into the dense and tangled jungle on my own! For today I had a truly TERRIFYING EXPERIENCE. This is what happened . . .

Humming a simple gorilla tune, I was swinging happily through the lower branches of the trees. I had travelled way beyond the outposts of the burly gorillas who keep guard over the city, and was enjoying being out on my own. The sun was filtering down through the leaves and birds were chirruping up above. I was just thinking what a beautiful and peaceful place the jungle could be when – *POW!*

Something exploded against my shoulder, knocking me from my branch and sending me spiralling to the forest floor.

You'd think after Twak had pounced on me I'd have leavnt my lesson by now!

I sat up slowly, rubbing my head and looking up into the branches. What had hit me? I looked at my shoulder and saw pawpaw juice running down my coat. The damaged fruit lay on the carpet of leaves close by. Perhaps it had just fallen from one of the trees, I thought, and stood up to brush myself down.

A hail of fruit and nuts cascaded from above, stinging my back, rapping against my skull and grazing my face! I leaped into the bushes, heart pounding in surprise and panic. What was going on?!

The jungle grew quiet again and I carefully parted the fronds of a giant fern and peered up into the trees.

Again a deluge of nuts, stones and fruit rained down and I threw myself to the ground, gritting my teeth as the projectiles bounced off me. They were really hard! Luckily I was wearing my coat, and I managed to pull the hood over my head to protect my face. Then I curled up in a ball and waited for the attack to stop. Eventually everything fell quiet again. I peeked out from under my hood and saw a slight movement. A shadowy form was stirring above me, its features hidden behind the curtain of leaves. What was it?

I waited for a long time, hoping that my hidden enemy had moved on. Hours passed in complete silence, and I finally decided that all was safe. I was just about to creep back onto the path, when—

'OOWAAA!'

A screaming face – a horrible face all purple
and blue – thrust through the foliage,
centimetres from my nose! I panicked and,
running as fast as I could, crashed through the
undergrowth as a million missiles ricocheted
from the trees and thumped into my back.

Whatever these vicious creatures were, I could
hear them clattering through the jungle behind me,
whooping and screaming and barking like savage
dogs.

'Clear off!' I yelled as I swung up through the
branches, climbing at top speed. 'Leave me
alone!'

The animals screamed in delight, hot on my
heels.

Then, as I scrambled into the top branches of
the trees, one lunged and sank sharp teeth into
my bottom.

'Yeagh!' I screamed, striking out blindly and
catching the animal across the snout, making it
release its hold.

I swung away faster than ever, racing through
the trees and praying that I could shake off these
fearsome attackers. I was sure that if they caught
me, I would never see home again. But, as I

neared Gorilla City, the creatures fell behind and then melted back into the jungle.

I've never been so grateful to see my gorilla friends swinging in the trees up ahead, but feeling shaken and slightly ashamed at how I'd fled from that weird painted face, I avoided everyone and climbed quickly up to my platform. Scared and exhausted, I flopped onto my bed.

Later

It's been a really horrible day. I'm going to try to get some sleep now. I just hope I won't have nightmares!

The Next Day

I've had horrible dreams full of painted faces that grinned at me like sneering tribal masks.

I don't think I'm ready to brave the jungle again on my own after all. I'm going to have to ask for help!

I dreamt of painted faces, like tribal masks

Bad News

I asked Grip and Grapple to help me find a way out of the jungle. They were really sad that I wanted to leave, but like the good friends they are they understood why I wanted to try. They suggested we ask the elders if they had ever heard of a way to leave. But the news wasn't good . . .

'Leave the jungle?' said Safner, a big male who leads the guards patrolling the perimeter of the city. 'No one leaves the jungle. It fills the whole of the world!'

'But it must finish somewhere,' I said, suddenly worried.

'Our city sits in the black heart of the impenetrable jungle, and the jungle stretches for hundreds of miles, until it reaches the walls at the end of the Earth,' explained Nanog, a really old female. 'You cannot climb these walls, for they rise, sheer and featureless, for a thousand metres. No one leaves the jungle.'

'But what's beyond the walls at the end of the earth?' I asked.

'The sky,' replied all the gorillas at once.

'But hasn't anyone ever tried to climb them?'

'Once, during the great flood,' said Nanog, 'a group of gorillas tried to climb to safety. But the climb was so dangerous that they fell to their deaths before they had reached halfway!'

Safner nodded. 'No one ever leaves the jungle,' he repeated emphatically.

'But if no one has climbed the cliffs, how do you know what lies beyond?' I protested.

'We don't need to climb them,' said Nanog, starting to get annoyed.

'We can see the sky perfectly well from the base of the cliffs!'

I sighed. So much for getting help! I was pretty sure that the gorillas were describing the sides to a steep gorge, like the one the waterfall had carried me over. And if the jungle is in a sunken valley, it might take me a hundred lifetimes to find a way out! But I'm *not* going to let my adventure end here. It's fun living with the gorillas, but I don't want to spend my whole life eating bananas and playing vine-tag! No matter how long it takes, I will find a way out. I *MUST* FIND A WAY OUT! I'll write more when I come up with a plan . . .

Really Bad News!

It's been a long, long time since I've written anything in this journal. I've been using every spare moment searching for a path that will lead me to the edge of the jungle. And I've certainly made some weird and wonderful discoveries.

The Trufflegrumper
The Trufflegrumper is a distant relative of the pig, and smells like a pile of rotting cabbage

leaves, only worse. It is meant to be delicious to eat, but it's so smelly that nothing can get near enough to catch it!

The Slimeball

A transparent blob of slime that creeps over the ground, digging shallow scoops in the earth in which to hide. Any unsuspecting animal that steps on one is stuck fast. The Slimeball, which has no mouth, then ingests the animal through

its skin, leaving its prey as a complete but hollow carcass. DO NOT STAND ON ONE!

But even though it's great to have discovered these strange animals, I've come no closer to finding a way out. Until today!

I was out with Grip and Grapple, exploring a part of the jungle that the gorillas rarely visit, when we found the cliff base! We were just swinging along, stretching our arms before breakfast, and suddenly,

Cliffs

Jungle.

me!

THERE IT WAS! A sheer wall of granite stretching away to left and right, and disappearing up above the thick foliage.

I whooped and thumped my chest with joy, and Grip and Grapple danced about, sharing my excitement. But when I bent my head back and looked up the steep cliff, my heart sank. The cliff-face rose high into the sky and I could see neither a handhold, nor the cliff top.

The gorillas had been right: I'd never be able to climb out. Not even with the best explorer kit in the world.

Grip and Grapple tried to cheer me up. 'Don't worry, you'll find a way out eventually,' they said. 'And, anyway, it's not so bad here, is it? The jungle's got everything a gorilla needs!'

And they were right, the jungle is a brilliant place. It provides me with food, water, shelter and friends. It has made me strong and fast and taught me what is good to eat and what is poisonous.

But at the end of the day, I am not a gorilla, I'm Charlie Small, and I don't belong here!

If a plant is bright ved and has spots, don't eat it!

So tomorrow I'm going to take a trip back to the cliff, and I'm going to follow it from one end of the valley to the other. I must find out if there's some way up, or if I'm really going to be trapped in the land of the apes for ever!

Really, Really Bad News!

I haven't been able to go back to the cliff after all. And I may never get the chance. Because something terrible has happened, and as king of the gorillas I must lead my tribe into battle!

This evening, as I was relaxing on my platform, Nanog, the old white gorilla, came and sat next to me. She seemed troubled.

'What's the matter, Nanog?' I asked.

'The mandrills are coming,' she said.

'Who on earth are the mandrills?'

'They are a tribe of blue-faced baboons that live in a far part of the jungle,' said Nanog, and a shudder ran down my spine. I knew straight away that these were the same vicious creatures that had attacked before.

'They are stupid, violent animals,' continued

the old gorilla. 'They do not store food for the lean times, and if the jungle harvest is poor, they go hungry. First they turn on themselves, and then they attack us. When the mandrills come, they steal and eat our young. They are smaller than us, but they are fast and aggressive and have muzzles full of huge teeth. Now our spies tell us that the mandrills have developed a taste for small pink gorillas and they are preparing a raid. How can that be?'

Small pink gorillas? I gulped.

'I did bump into some creatures with blue faces,' I admitted, rubbing my bottom. 'But that was ages ago.'

'The mandrills never forget, Charlie,' said Nanog with a worried frown. 'It seems that the one who bit you has told his clan how wonderful small pink gorillas taste. They are plotting to come and capture you. And many of our young. What are we to do?'

How was I supposed to know? I was just a small boy, alone in a jungle many miles from home. But then I remembered: I was also the gorilla king, and it was my job to know. Well, one thing was certain, I wasn't going to offer myself up as a starter at a mandrill feast! And there was no way those blue-faced monkeys were going to eat any of my friends!

'We must stand up to them,' I said. 'We have to teach them a lesson they'll never forget.'

Nanog didn't look convinced.

'How long have we got before they come?' I asked.

'They've already been seen near our city,' said Nanog as she stood up to leave. 'We think they will attack within the week. You must think of a plan, Charlie!'

As I watched the old gorilla swing off through the trees, I began to realize what being a king was really about. The whole tribe was relying on me to keep them safe.

But if the gorillas didn't know how to defeat their old enemies, how would I be able to save the day?

Prepare For Attack

I sat alone through the night, staring at the stars scattered across the sky, trying to think of a way to save my friends (and myself!). By morning I had a plan.

I felt it was my fault that the mandrills were coming, and so I decided I should face them alone. After all, it was a pink gorilla they particularly wanted! I also thought that if one small, hairless gorilla could stand up to them, the mandrills might think twice before ever attacking our city again.

The gorillas weren't very happy with this idea. They said they wouldn't just stand by and watch such a deadly enemy attack me. But when I explained that I planned to lure the mandrills into a trap, they agreed to follow my lead.

First I instructed the gorillas to plait leaves and fronds and make a huge net. Then we bent hoops of bamboo into the ground beneath the city, and laid the long net on top of them. I had learned that the mandrills are natural ground dwellers, and I knew they would try and force me down from the treetops and fight on their home turf, and I wanted to turn their schemes against them.

We camouflaged the net with leaves and, using smaller and smaller hoops, created a long, hidden tunnel that gradually got narrower and narrower, until it ended in a

small exit hole with a drawstring attached.
This is what it looked like:

I felt pretty confident that we could catch the
mandrills in it. But I wasn't at all sure if I'd be
fast enough to lead them into the trap before
they could catch and eat me. Before I had a
chance to practise swinging from the city down
to the forest floor, a warning alarm sounded.
The enemy had been spotted in the trees near
the city!

A Rumble In The Jungle

I just had time to climb to the ceremonial
platform when the mandrills appeared, their red

Netting will be camouflaged.)

Netting

← In

and blue faces materializing silently amongst the foliage.

My tribe had hidden themselves below, some in lower branches, some down on the ground, so I faced the enemy alone and pounded my chest as hard as I could.

'Here I am!' I bellowed. 'Come and get me!' A large bull male reared up, baring his teeth, and with a scream the mandrills attacked. A swarm of them poured out of the trees, leaping for the platform and driving me down from the treetops.

Blimey, were they fast! I dropped, crashing

through the leaves, only grabbing a branch occasionally to check my fall. The mandrills followed, barking and snapping their jaws.

As I hit the ground running, one beast was almost upon me! I could feel its hot breath on my back and hear its panting snarls. If it hadn't been for one of my gorillas reaching out a powerful arm from a hiding place to send the mandrill flying, it would have all been over for me!

I heard a muffled cry as my pursuer sailed into the undergrowth, and I ran full pelt to the entrance of our trap.

The other mandrills followed, fast as greyhounds, pouring into the camouflaged tunnel behind me. As it narrowed, I had to crouch, then run on all fours, with the mandrills snarling and snapping at my heels.

When the last of them had entered the tunnel, the gorillas dashed from the undergrowth, growling and beating their chests, driving their enemies deeper into the trap.

I reached the end of the tunnel just in time, squeezed through the tiny exit and pulled on the drawstring, closing and tying it behind me.

The mandrills at the front of the pack

couldn't turn round in the narrow tunnel, and the rest piled in behind, squashing the lot into a tightly packed mass of frantic, screaming animals.

The gorillas quickly fastened the tunnel at the other end and we had them. Every last one!

We dragged the huge wriggling net back along the jungle paths to the mandrills' distant village. The rest of their clan came out to watch as we dumped our catch in a heap.

Our message was clear. We had trapped the mighty mandrill warriors as easily as we might collect a bag full of fruit.

Then I climbed atop the net and, baring my teeth and thumping my chest, roared: '*Nnga mowee mmwa mwa. Woopopomwadoomwa nyo!*' (You have been warned. Attack us again at your peril. The war is over!)

The mandrills squeaked in terrified agreement, and we knew that they'd never trouble Gorilla City again.

Run Away! Run Away!

We're back from the mandrill village and a huge celebration is underway. Everyone is dancing

113

and singing on the platforms below me, but I don't really feel like joining in. You see, the gorillas have insisted on rewarding me for leading them to victory. And I really don't want to accept their gift.

At first I thought they were going to give me some sort of medal, but then Nanog introduced me to a huge gorilla wearing a garland of purple flowers on her head.

To begin with I didn't quite understand why the old gorilla wanted me to meet her. Then I realized – she was presenting me to her daughter, the lovely (but also incredibly hairy) Grunter. My reward is to be her hand in marriage!

Yikes!

What was I supposed to do? I knew that to refuse would be a terrible insult, but there was no way I was going to

This is the lovely Grunter,

My intended!

marry anyone. I'm much too young to get married! Especially to someone with armpit hair as long as my leg!

So I greeted her as politely as I could, then, with a big yawn, I pretended to be exhausted from the fight with the mandrills, and climbed up to my platform.

Now, lying here on my banana-leaf bed, I've decided I can't possibly stay another night. I've made some very good friends amongst the gorillas and I feel really sad to be leaving Grip and Grapple. But enough is enough, and marrying one of them is going too far!

I've decided to slip away quietly before dawn tomorrow, because I'm worried that if I tell anyone my plans they might decide to bring the date of the wedding forward.

I'll write more if I manage to sneak away!

A Fellow Explorer

At last I seem to be having some good luck! I managed to sneak away unnoticed this morning, and I've made it all the way to the cliff-face without being followed. Even better, I've made a brilliant discovery – although quite a grisly one!

I'd been walking along the cliff-bottom, desperately searching for a way up, when I spotted a man leaning against the rocks. I could see he'd been there for quite some time because even though his pith helmet and walking boots were still in place, his bones were bleached white by the sun.

Gingerly, I crept up to the skeleton. The remains of a safari jacket were hanging in tatters from his bony shoulders. And the remains of a rotting leather water bottle hung across one shoulder.

I didn't want to get too close, but I knew that I should check to see if he was carrying anything useful. Carefully, I felt through his pockets, and discovered some brilliant stuff:

A compass

A torch (wind up)

A very sharp hunting knife

A slab of Kendal Mint Cake (as carried to the summit of Mount Everest in 1953)

Jungle

Some diarrhoea tablets (who knows when they might come in handy?)

And best of all, still gripped in his bone-white fingers, was a map. A map that showed a route out of the valley, by way of a hidden pass! I was less than an hour's walk from a way out of the jungle at last.

Home, here I come!

This is the very map that I found:

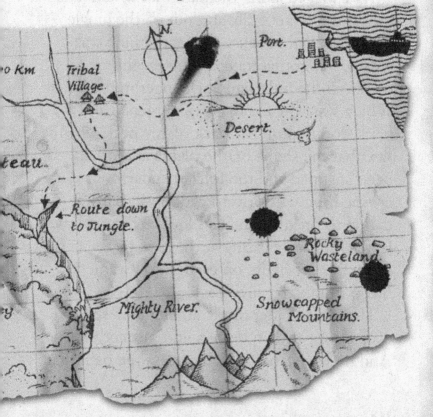

We Meet Again

But, oh no! I'm not at home. I am probably further away from home than ever, in a position even more precarious than the jungle valley. I am in chains, in the middle of an ocean, and my life is in the hands of . . . well, let me explain what has happened.

As I walked along the path that would take me up the secret gully and out of the jungle valley, I began to sense that something was wrong. My gorilla training had taught me to notice all the little signs of danger in the jungle. Which was why my muscles tightened and the hairs stood up on the back of my neck when I saw that the stems of the plants ahead had been snapped and the foliage underfoot crushed. I crept forward cautiously, hardly daring to breathe, and as I looked through the leaves into the clearing at the base of the cliffs, I saw the last figure on earth that I wanted to meet: Thrak, the silverback!

He looked older but if anything he seemed even stronger than before, and meaner too. And he was standing right across the path that would take me to freedom.

I decided to try and work my way around him and join the path further along.

Inch by inch, I made my way around the clearing, crouching low behind the bushes and rocks that littered the ground at the cliff base. My eyes never left Thrak as he busied himself scrabbling for termites and scratching his dusty hide. Just as I had passed him and could step back onto the path beyond, an animal crashed through the undergrowth beside me with a loud, piteous bellow. Typical. It was a Great Hairy Wazzock, another creature that I had named. And this one was really living up to its reputation!

Just so you know, this is what one of these beasts looks like:

The Great Hairy Wazzock

A ridiculous-looking animal of the antelope family. Unlike most antelopes, the wazzock is a forest dweller, rather slow and very clumsy. Although his long hair should offer perfect camouflage amongst the trees, the wazzock is bright pink in colour and so easy prey for the jungle panthers.

The noise made Silverback spin round, and his face split into a grin as he saw me trying to hide amongst the low bushes.

'So, we meet again, hairless monkey,' he said, leaning casually against the trunk of a tree. Having spent so long amongst the jungle gorillas, I could easily understand his guttural grunts. 'And this time your striped power berries won't save you,' he added.

'You were beaten fair and square,' I said. 'Any gorilla who can't take the heat of an old mint humbug doesn't deserve to be king of the apes. You're nothing more than a bully, a great big fraud, a sissy, a—'

The silverback roared and lunged at me. But I was faster. I swung up onto a branch and somersaulted over his head. 'So long, sucker!' I laughed, grinning over my shoulder as I sprinted down the path.

I was still grinning when my foot slipped on a loose rock and tumbled me into the dirt.

Thrak was on me in an instant.

'So, I'm a sissy, am I?' he spluttered into my face.

'Phoar!' I gasped. 'Haven't you heard of flossing, compost breath?' Which was probably even stupider than falling over the rock! Because, with a mighty roar of indignation, Thrak picked me up in one hand and, spinning like an Olympic discus thrower, launched me high into the air.

I sailed above the top of the jungle and, in a blur of green and blue, streaked across the sky at what seemed like a hundred miles an hour.

I glimpsed flashes of sky, then, tumbling through the air like an out-of-control acrobat, I spotted sea and then sand, and then—

Boing! I bounced off a vast bed of spongy seaweed floating on the surface of the sea, and landed, quite unharmed, on the white sands of a palm-fringed beach.

Where Am I now?

I sat dazed and dizzy from my gorilla-propelled flight and waited for my head to clear. After a few moments I got to my feet and looked around.

Where was I now? I couldn't believe that stupid great interfering silverback had ruined my chances of getting home! The bony explorer's map would be useless now. Sure, it showed me the way out of the jungle. But now I was nowhere near the jungle!

Instead, I seemed to be on a small island, one end of which was covered with palm trees, the other rising to a rocky hill. With a heavy sigh, I decided the best thing to do was climb the hill and get my bearings, so I scrambled through the scrubby bushes that fringed its base and started to climb the rocky outcrop. I was soon standing on the top of the hill.

I could see straight away that the island was almost completely circular, with tall cliffs rising vertically out of a rock-strewn sea. I had, rather luckily,

Rocky Outcrop

Scrub

Beach

Cannon

Bay

Seaweed

landed on the only stretch of beach on the island, bordering the sea in a hidden harbour that was almost encircled by steep, rocky headlands. Anyone wishing to defend this island would find it a very easy task.

And defend the island is what somebody was obviously prepared to do, for when I walked out along one of the bluffs, I discovered a great cannon overlooking the entrance to the

This is the Island
I landed on

Fortification

Palm Trees

ake

Sheer cliffs

Sea

bay. There was a pyramid of cannonballs and a strongbox filled with gunpowder alongside it. And I could see a similar cannon at the end of the opposite bluff.

I looked around nervously. Cannons meant people, but they also meant people expecting trouble. And people who might not like a visit from a boy who'd arrived out of nowhere! I felt sure I was being watched – it was the same prickly feeling I'd had when I first entered the jungle all those months ago. But surely there were no grumpy silverbacks on this tiny island?

I decided not to take any chances until I'd investigated the whole place. So I scrambled down from the hilltop and crept quietly along the fringe of trees on the beach. Then, almost invisible, hidden amongst the vegetation, I spotted a solid timber wall.

The wall was made of massive logs lashed together and was over three metres high. Creeping along it, I discovered a pair of thick wooden gates. I pushed gently against them, but they were shut fast. Then I spotted a crack between the logs and, peering through, saw a sandy compound, but no sign of life. It was deserted.

Still with the uneasy feeling that I wasn't alone, I took the long scarf out of my rucksack and knotted one end, which I threw over the top of the wall. The knot caught between two of the sharpened logs. Pulling on the other end of my scarf to make sure it was secure, I scrambled up over the wall and jumped down into the compound.

Knot held in V of Posts

Scarf

How I used my scarf to help me climb the fortress wall

On the far side was a lean-to building and I hurried up and tried the door. It was also locked but, looking through the dirtiest of its windows, I could see a table laden with amazing food! There were cured meats, salamis and loaves of bread, pickles and pies and pastries. I groaned. Food! Real food!

I suddenly realized how hungry I was. I hadn't eaten anything since yesterday and I had only eaten leaves, shoots and fruit throughout my time with the gorillas. My tummy growled in anticipation and I decided that even if it was stealing, I had to have a thick ham doorstop sandwich.

I got out the strong hunting knife that I had found on the bony explorer and slipped it through the gap in the window frame. Sliding the blade up, I managed to lift the clasp on the window and it swung open. Without a moment's hesitation and not bothering to check if I was being observed, I scrambled through the window and dropped into the room on the other side.

A Feast Fit For A King

I ran straight to the table and, pulling back a chair, sat down to a wonderful spread. I grabbed the loaf, not bothering to wonder at how fresh it was, ripped off a chunk and topped it with two thick slices of ham. These I smeared with pickle, adding sliced tomato, salami and cheese, and took a huge bite.

It was absolutely delicious, but not enough! I spied a cold turkey leg and devoured that. I ate a whole pheasant pie and a plate of what might have been blubbery whale meat. I drank a tankard of foaming brown ale, which I poured from a barrel in the corner, and finished it all off with a large slice of soggy bread pudding.

Pushing my plate away, I gave a satisfied belch and yawned. I'd eaten rather more than I had planned and I was starting to feel very tired. I hoped the owners wouldn't mind me helping myself, but it was too late to worry now, so I decided to look around and try and find out who lived here.

They were certainly an untidy lot. Plates were unwashed, knives left speared in the table and the floor littered with scraps of rotting food. The bedroom was no better. Hung with a rows of hammocks, it was piled with filthy clothes that smelled like a skunk with a tummy upset. On a windowsill lay a row of large whale teeth, all intricately engraved with pictures of sailing ships and sea monsters. I decided the inhabitants were probably whalers or fishermen.

Then I discovered a heavy padlocked door.

The owners were obviously determined that no one would go beyond it, because the padlocks secured a row of bolts that ran all the way around the entrance. There didn't seem to be any other way through, but there was a small barred opening near the top of the door.

I couldn't help wondering what had to be kept so securely locked up. Something valuable perhaps? Something dangerous? Maybe a desperate prisoner! With another mighty yawn I clambered onto a stool and peered through the bars. It was very dark inside, and at first I couldn't see a thing. But as my eyes grew accustomed to the gloom, I started to make out some vague shapes. There was a stack of old crates or boxes piled against the far wall; some rolls of cloth, dusty and cobwebbed, and piles of metal that glowed dully in the gloom. By the door a stack of shelves carried volumes of atlases and charts, and very near the grating through which I was peering was another, smaller roll of cloth.

I threaded my arm through the bars and stretched. My fingers could just touch the roll, and by scratching and scrabbling I managed to ease it forward until it fell into my hand. As I pulled the cloth back through the bars, I happened to glance down, and there, just below me, on the other side of the door, stood another of the crates. But this crate had split open, and from the inside a cascade of gold coins, goblets, diamonds and rubies had spilt across the floor.

I'd found a treasure trove! A stash of filched contraband! My heart started to pound as I rushed over to the dinner table and unrolled the piece of cloth in my hand, already knowing what I would find.

The Jolly Roger!

My legs started to wobble and I collapsed into a chair. I had to get out of this place – and quickly! But even as I sat there, I was overcome with fatigue. I don't know whether it was the huge meal I had just eaten, or the excitement of my flight from the jungle valley, but all of a sudden I just couldn't keep my eyes open and despite the great danger I was in, I fell into a deep, deep sleep.

A Rude Awakening

I don't know how long I slept for, but all of a sudden the door to the building burst open. I awoke with a start, blinking at the bright light that flooded in from outside.

A group of burly figures were silhouetted in the doorway and as they edged towards me, I saw cutlasses flash in their hands.

I swallowed hard. I was in really serious trouble this time. I was faced with a gang of the most gruesome and grisly cut-throats imaginable. Their arms were ringed with jewelled bangles and their necks laden with golden chains. And from their tricorn hats to their grubby boots, they were loaded with

Woops. Missed a Page!

weapons: swords, pistols, cudgels and daggers.

There was no doubt about it. I was caught in a den of terrible bloodthirsty renegade pirates. And worst of all: they were all women!

Publisher's note:
This is where the first notebook ends.

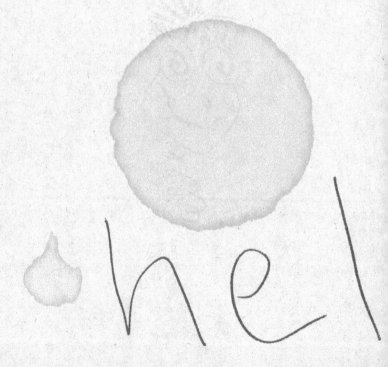

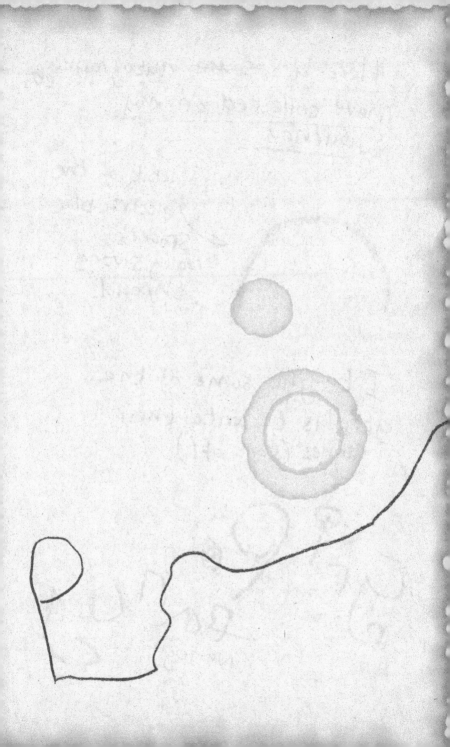

Here are some autographs etc.
I have collected on my
journey.

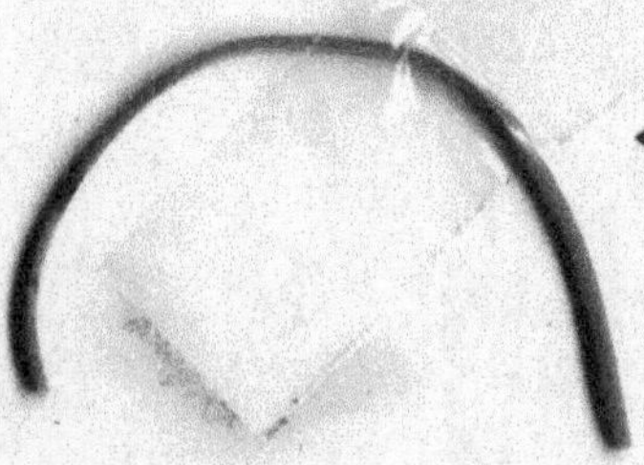

A bit of the
electric blue
spider's
really strong
thread.

I taught some of the
gorillas to write their
names (sort of!)

(Nanog)

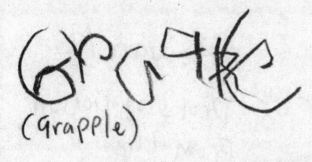

(grapple)

Some hair
from the ←
hyena

_ The paw-print
of a ~~Charlie~~
charliesmallicus
(it ran over
my open
book).

Beware!!

← Drops of Poison
from the
giant snake.
Do not lick!

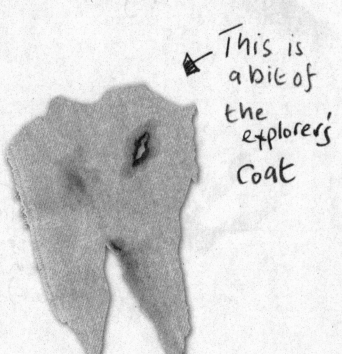

← This is
a bit of
the
explorer's
coat

I think this
must be Thrak's signature!!
I saw him looking through
my journal one morning, and
he must have done it then!

PREDATOR RATING 12

THRAK

A big, bone-headed silverback gorilla with huge muscles and a brain the size of a pea. Best weapons of defence: Mints and brain power.

WILD ANIMAL COLLECTOR'S CARD

My design for a new wild animal collector's card!